ONCE UPON A BANANA

Jennifer Armstrong
Illustrated by David Small

Simon & Schuster Books for Young Readers · New York · London · Toronto · Sydney

For K. R. and N. S.
—J. A.

To Lily Roan
—D. S.

SIMON & SCHUSTER BOOKS FOR YOUNG READERS · An imprint of Simon & Schuster Children's Publishing Division · 1230 Avenue of the Americas, New York, New York 10020 · Text copyright © 2006 by Jennifer Armstrong · Illustrations copyright © 2006 by David Small · All rights reserved, including the right of reproduction in whole or in part in any form. · SIMON & SCHUSTER BOOKS FOR YOUNG READERS is a trademark of Simon & Schuster, Inc. · Book design by Dan Potash and Jessica Sonkin · The text for this book is set in Alcoholica. · The illustrations for this book are rendered in watercolor. · Manufactured in China · 10 9 8 7 6 5 4 3 2 1 · Library of Congress Cataloging-in-Publication Data · Armstrong, Jennifer, 1961– · Once upon a banana / Jennifer Armstrong ; illustrated by David Small. · p. cm. · Summary: Everyday signs serve as captions for this pictorial tale of what happens after a monkey tosses a banana peel into the garbage can and misses. · ISBN-13: 978-0-689-84251-1 · ISBN-10: 0-689-84251-1 · [1. Bananas—Fiction. 2. Signs and signboards—Fiction. 3. Humorous stories.] · I. Small, David, 1945– ill. II. Title. PZ7.A73367On 2006 · [E]—dc22 · 2005008567

PLEASE
PUT LITTER
IN ITS
PLACE

LOADING
ZONE

KEY

A. Please Put Litter in Its Place
B. No Parking in This Space
C. Caution! Wet Paint!
D. Office of Complaint
E. 4-Way Stop
F. Barber Shop
G. One-Way Street
H. No Bare Feet
I. City Hall

J. Shopping Mall
K. Underpass
L. Keep Off the Grass!
M. Speed Bump
N. To the Dump
O. Public Phone
P. Loading Zone
Q. Look Both Ways
R. Have a Nice Day!